ouch!

READY STEADY READ

Sticker Fun!

Make reading fun with the Ready Steady Read series of books!

Once you've read the story, complete the activities at the back by using the stickers opposite. The stickers are reusable, so you can do the activities again and again!

E.g. The nest was too (**small**).

Check your answers at the back of the book. Once you've done each activity correctly, stick a star on your reading tree. Well done!

There are also some stickers just for you!

Ready?
Steady?
Let's read!

This
READY STEADY READ
book belongs to:

My Reading Tree!

To Sally, with love — R S

To Mark, from a grateful dad — M T

LITTLE TIGER PRESS
An imprint of Magi Publications
1 The Coda Centre, 189 Munster Road,
London SW6 6AW
www.littletigerpress.com

First published in Great Britain 2006
This edition published 2008

Text copyright © Ragnhild Scamell 2006
Illustrations copyright © Michael Terry 2006
Ragnhild Scamell and Michael Terry have asserted
their rights to be identified as the author and
illustrator of this work under the Copyright,
Designs and Patents Act, 1988.

A CIP catalogue record for this book is available
from the British Library.

Printed in China

10 9 8 7 6 5 4 3 2 1

Ragnhild Scamell

Illustrated by

Michael Terry

ouch!

LITTLE TIGER PRESS
London

Hedgehog had just finished building her winter nest under the old apple tree. Not too large and not too small. Just right for a nice, long winter sleep.

Plop!  Suddenly a juicy, red
apple landed on
her back.

"Ouch!" squeaked
Hedgehog. She
curled into a spiny
ball, hoping it
would fall off. But
when she uncurled,
the juicy, red apple
was still there.

Hedgehog tried to squeeze herself
and the apple into the beautiful, new
nest. But could she get in? No.
She could not. Not with the
apple on her back. The
nest was too small.

Oh dear!

Squirrel, scurrying past with an armful of brown nuts, stopped to help.

"Stand still. I'll push the apple off," he said.

And he pushed. And he struggled.

And he heaved. And he tugged.

But the juicy, red apple stayed where it was. Worse still, three of Squirrel's brown nuts got caught in Hedgehog's spines. So now she had a juicy, red apple and three brown nuts on her back.

"Oh dear!" wailed Hedgehog. "Winter is coming and I can't get into my nest. What will I do?"

"Try rolling on your back," snorted Pig, trotting up. "That'll get rid of it all."

Hedgehog threw herself
on the ground. Her little
legs paddled in the air as
she twisted and wriggled
and rolled.

"Has it all gone?" she asked hopefully, scrabbling to her feet.

Pig shook his head. No. The juicy, red apple and the three brown nuts were still there. So were a small, green pear and a crumpled, brown leaf.

"Oh dear," sighed Hedgehog, rolling her eyes.

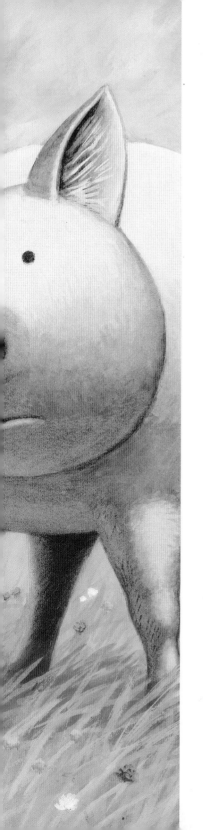

But up in the sky, sailing towards Hedgehog, she saw a colourful bit of card.

"Bother!" she cried.

This way and that she ran, as fast as she could.

This way and that drifted the card . . .

. . . and landed right
on her back, between
the apple and the
three brown nuts.

"It's not fair!" cried
Hedgehog, who now
had a juicy, red apple,
three brown nuts,
a small, green pear, a
crumpled, brown leaf
and a colourful bit of
card on her back.
"I'll never get into
my nest!"

Hedgehog pattered to the pond and gazed at her reflection in the water.

"Hello, Hedgehog. That's a lot of stuff on your back," croaked Frog.

"Hmph! I'm trying to get rid of it," sniffed Hedgehog.

"Dive," said Frog.

"That will wash it off."

Hedgehog dipped a foot in the murky water, then dived.

Splash! Her friends watched Hedgehog bobbing up and down. The juicy, red apple, the three brown nuts, the small, green pear, the crumpled, brown leaf and the colourful bit of card were all still there.
So was a pink water lily.

"Glug-glug-glug," gurgled
Hedgehog as the others heaved
her out of the water. She did
look funny!

But Hedgehog did not find it funny.
"Stop laughing!" she spluttered
and stamped her feet on the ground.
"Where am I going to sleep?"
Pig and Squirrel looked worried.
So did Frog.

"I do have one last idea," oinked Pig. "Squeeze through that hedge over there. That'll brush everything off."

So Hedgehog closed her eyes and squeezed herself through the thick leaves. But did it get everything off her back?

No! It did not. It was all still there.
So were four ripe blackberries.
And staring at her, with a look
of great surprise, stood Goat!

"Oooh!" cried Goat. "You've brought LUNCH!"

"Help yourself," said Hedgehog. "Take it all."

"Yippee!" brayed Goat.

Then he picked off and ate the juicy, red apple, the three brown nuts, the small, green pear, the pink water lily and the four ripe blackberries.

For pudding, he ate the card. The only thing he left was the crumpled, brown leaf. He just couldn't eat any more.

"Hoorah!" cried Hedgehog. She felt as light as a feather. "Thank you, Goat," she said.

Then she ran, as fast as her little legs could carry her, home to her nest.

Hedgehog squeezed into her little nest.
It fitted her perfectly! And it was the
best nest ever. Outside a cold wind
blew another apple off the tree. But
it didn't fall on Hedgehog. She was
safe in her nest and fast, fast asleep.

 # Picture Dictionary

Look at the words below and put the correct picture stickers next to each word.

apple   blackberry

leaf   nut

★ Have you got these right?
Then put a star on your reading tree!

 # Groovy Groups

Each **Groovy Groups** word sticker is either an animal, colour or season. Look at the groups of words below and stick the word stickers in the correct group.

Animals		
hedgehog frog pig	_____	_____

Colours		
red brown green	_____	_____

Seasons	
spring summer autumn	_____

★ Did you put the words in the right group?
Then add another star to your reading tree!

Simple Sentences

These sentences from the story have been split in the middle and muddled up! Draw a line to join them up again. We've done the first one for you.

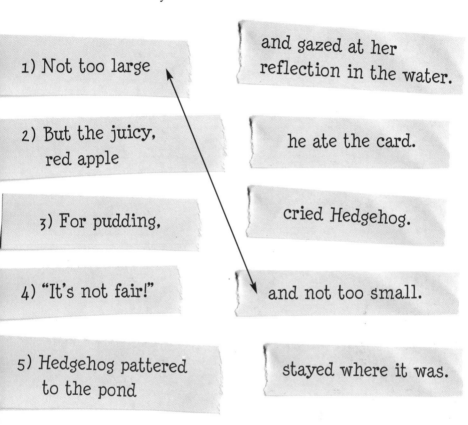

1) Not too large

and gazed at her reflection in the water.

2) But the juicy, red apple

he ate the card.

3) For pudding,

cried Hedgehog.

4) "It's not fair!"

and not too small.

5) Hedgehog pattered to the pond

stayed where it was.

★ Did you get this right? Remember to add another star to your reading tree!

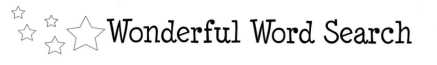# Wonderful Word Search

Find the following ten words in the word search below.
The words can be found written down and across.

caught	murky	funny
ouch	gone	reflection
heaved	sleep	
lunch	under	

M	U	R	K	Y	Z	S	U	H	W
W	A	C	L	N	O	J	B	X	U
R	E	F	L	E	C	T	I	O	N
Y	J	D	U	L	F	C	Y	I	D
K	H	P	N	R	E	M	N	C	E
V	E	G	C	A	U	G	H	T	R
Q	A	S	H	U	X	O	E	G	K
H	V	U	A	W	R	N	A	H	O
L	E	P	T	S	L	E	E	P	U
B	D	N	F	O	Z	D	X	V	C
O	P	T	F	U	N	N	Y	I	H

Can you find these words in the story?

★ When you have done the word search,
add a star to your reading tree!

 # Amazing Adjectives

An **adjective** is a describing word. Add the missing adjectives to the sentences from the story below using the word stickers.

> spiny – crumpled – cold – juicy – murky

1) Suddenly a _____ , red apple landed on Hedgehog's back.

2) Hedgehog dipped a foot in the _____ water.

3) She curled into a _____ ball, hoping it would fall off.

4) The only thing he left was the _____ brown leaf.

5) Outside a _____ wind blew another apple off the tree.

Can you find these sentences in the story?

★ Did you get all the adjectives right? Great!
Add another star to your reading tree.

Past Tense

A **verb** is a doing word. If a verb describes something that has already happened, it is in the **past tense**. Some verbs end in **-ed** to show that they are in the past tense.

Look at the sentences below. Underline the verbs in the past tense.

1) "Try rolling on your back," snorted Pig.
2) Suddenly a juicy, red apple landed on her back.
3) "Stop laughing!" she spluttered.
4) Hedgehog pattered to the pond and gazed at her reflection in the water.
5) "I do have one last idea," oinked Pig.

★ Did you get this right? Remember to add another star to your reading tree!

Drawing

Let's get creative! Draw a picture in the frame for each word below.

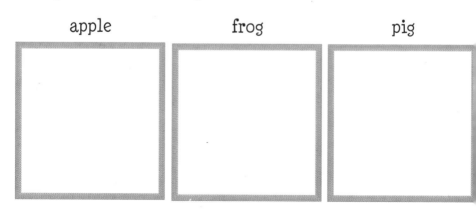

apple	frog	pig

★ Did you draw all three pictures?
Add the last star to your reading tree!

Reading is Fun!

Notes for Parents

Helping your child learn to read can be lots of fun!
Here are some tips to help:

Make reading time a special time you spend together.
Let your child choose their own books to read.
When reading a story, try using different voices for different characters.
Talk about the story and the pictures in the book, and point things out.
Read favourite stories again and again.
Encourage your child to join in.
Use the story to encourage your child to talk about their feelings.
When your child is confident, ask them if they'd like to read the story to you.
Remember to praise and encourage your child at all times.

Answers

Past Tense

1) snorted 2) landed 3) spluttered
4) pattered; gazed 5) oinked

Amazing Adjectives

1) juicy 2) murky 3) spiny
4) crumpled 5) cold

Wonderful Word Search

H	I	Y	N	N	F	T	P	O
C	V	X	D	N	F	O	Z	B
U	E	E	E	S	T	L	E	P
O	H	V	N	R	W	A	V	U
K	G	E	U	X	H	S	A	Q
R	T	H	G	U	A	C	G	V
E	C	N	W	E	R	N	P	H	K
I	Y	C	F	L	U	J	D	Y
N	O	I	T	C	E	L	F	E	R
U	X	B	J	N	L	C	A	W
W	H	U	S	Z	Y	R	U	M

Simple Sentences

1) Not too large — and not too small.
2) But the juicy, red apple — stayed where it was.
3) For pudding, — he ate the card.
4) "It's not fair!" — cried Hedgehog.
5) Hedgehog pattered to the pond — and gazed at her reflection in the water.

Groovy Groups

Animals: goat; squirrel
Colours: pink; blue
Seasons: winter

Picture Dictionary

 leaf
 nut
 apple
 blackberry

Ready Steady Read

SIX new titles in this great series!

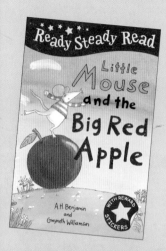

Ready Steady Read

Little Mouse and the Big Red Apple

A.H. Benjamin and Gwyneth Williamson

Ready Steady Read

Mouse, Mole and the Falling Star

Ready Steady Read

The BIGGEST BADDEST WOLF

Nick Ward

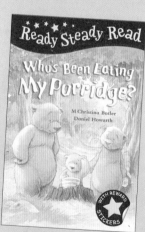

Ready Steady Read

Who's Been Eating My Porridge?

M Christina Butler
Daniel Howarth

Ready Steady Read

Nobody Laughs at a Lion!

Paul Bright
Illustrated by Matt Buckingham

Ready Steady Read

ROBOT DOG

[REJECT]

MARK OLIVER

For information regarding any of the above
titles or for our catalogue, please contact us:
Little Tiger Press, 1 The Coda Centre,
189 Munster Road, London SW6 6AW
Tel: 020 7385 6333 Fax: 020 7385 7333
E-mail: info@littletiger.co.uk • www.littletigerpress.com